Born in 1959, one of n̲   ̲.̲.̲.̲y̲s̲ been a constant for David. He ̲ ̲.̲.̲.̲ ̲his career as a conservation forester, undoubtedly influenced by a deep love for the outdoors. When not working to protect woodlands, he can be found telling stories to his three young girls, aged 12, 9 and 7. David's practical skills extend beyond forestry, as a certified instructor, assessor in forestry operations. Despite a non-academic background, he possesses a remarkable vocabulary and a vivid imagination, perhaps fuelled by countless hours spent exploring untamed landscapes.

David Price

THE STING OF THE BIRCH, A WHISPER FROM GOD

AUSTIN MACAULEY PUBLISHERS
LONDON • CAMBRIDGE • NEW YORK • SHARJAH

Copyright © David Price 2025

The right of David Price to be identified as author of this work has been asserted by the author in accordance with sections 77 and 78 of the Copyright, Designs and Patents Act 1988.

All rights reserved. No part of this publication may be reproduced, stored in a retrieval system, or transmitted in any form or by any means, electronic, mechanical, photocopying, recording, or otherwise, without the prior permission of the publishers.

Any person who commits any unauthorised act in relation to this publication may be liable to criminal prosecution and civil claims for damages.

This is a work of fiction. Names, characters, businesses, places, events, locales, and incidents are either the products of the author's imagination or used in a fictitious manner. Any resemblance to actual persons, living or dead, or actual events is purely coincidental.

A CIP catalogue record for this title is available from the British Library.

ISBN 9781035878307 (Paperback)
ISBN 9781035878314 (ePub e-book)

www.austinmacauley.com

First Published 2025
Austin Macauley Publishers Ltd®
1 Canada Square
Canary Wharf
London
E14 5AA

Table of Contents

Foreword	7
Chapter 1: The Weight of the Birch	9
Chapter 2: A Cold Whisper of Comfort	12
Chapter 3: A Whisper of Rebellion	16
Chapter 4: Echoes of Another World	20
Chapter 5: A Price for Silence	24
Chapter 6: The Price of Inaction	28
Chapter 7: Beyond the Veil	31
Chapter 8: The Price of Conviction	33
Chapter 9: Supper of Shadows	35
Chapter 10: Desolation's Embrace	37
Chapter 11: A Song of Redemption	39
Chapter 12: Whispers on the Wind	42
Chapter 13: Unveiling the Maker	45
Chapter 14: Whispers of the Soul	49
Chapter 15: A Newfound Vulnerability	52

Foreword

Have you ever glimpsed a flicker of cruelty behind a pious smile? Sister Agnes, the convent's serene disciplinarian, embodies this disturbing duality. Beneath her starched wimple and unwavering gaze lies a secret as dark and twisted as the birch rod she wields with chilling righteousness. *The Sting of the Birch, a Whisper from God* is not your grandmother's sermon.

It's a heart-pounding exploration of faith, twisted penance, and the terrifying unknown that waits beyond the veil of life. Prepare to enter a world where devotion curdles into sadism, and the price of redemption seems far bleaker than any earthly punishment. But beyond the convent's shadowed halls lies another realm – a dimension where the tapestry of our lives is meticulously rewoven. Here, not just sins are laid bare, but the quiet joys we nurtured and the good deeds we sowed also find their reckoning. Will Sister Agnes discover solace in this celestial judgment, or will the darkness she harbours condemn her to an eternity of suffering?

Crack open this book, and step into the hallowed halls of the convent. But remember, this chilling journey transcends the boundaries of mortality. It's here, on the precipice of the afterlife, that Sister Agnes' fate – and perhaps yours – will be truly decided.

Chapter 1
The Weight of the Birch

~*~

The aged floorboards creaked beneath Sister Agnes' brisk steps as she hurried down the dim hallway. Her starched wimple brushed against the rough stone wall, a stark contrast to the practiced serenity etched on her face. Today was Agnes' favourite day – judgement day for young Sister Clara, a bright-eyed novice with a smile that grated on Agnes' nerves. Clara, a recent arrival, was a breath of fresh air in the stoic monastery. Her bright eyes, unlike the downcast gazes of the other novices, held a spark of defiance, a youthful optimism that grated on Agnes. News of Clara's arrival had preceded her, whispers of a girl with a rebellious spirit, a laugh that echoed too brightly in the hallowed halls. Agnes, ever the stern disciplinarian, had braced herself for this confrontation – but also, with a sickening twist, prepared herself for a new opportunity.

Clara's journey to the monastery wasn't one of pure devotion. Unlike Agnes, whose path had been paved by a sheltered upbringing and a yearning for order, Clara's reasons were shrouded in mystery. Rumours swirled – some said she sought refuge from a broken heart, others that a family tragedy had driven her to seek solace in the rigid structure of the monastery. Whatever her reasons, Clara's arrival had disrupted the carefully curated tranquillity of Agnes' world. Her smile, a beacon of something unfamiliar, challenged the very foundation of Agnes' self-imposed control. It was a defiance, Agnes saw not as a threat to the monastery's order, but as a delicious invitation. Clara, with her innocent spirit and untamed will, was like a lamb led to the slaughter – a new victim for Agnes' sadistic desires, cleverly disguised as holy duty. Reaching the heavy oak door, Agnes paused. A bead of sweat trickled down her temple, a physical betrayal of the calm she projected. Was it the weight of the birch rod clutched in her hand, or the gnawing guilt that always accompanied this ritual? She banished the thought with a silent prayer. This was penance. For Clara's disobedience, yes, but also for the dark pleasure that bloomed within Agnes with each rhythmic strike. Taking a deep breath, Agnes rapped sharply on the door. The anticipation was almost unbearable, a sickening mix of piety and a thrill that made her fingers itch for the cool touch of the polished wood. A timid voice called out from within, and with a practiced smile, Agnes pushed open the door, ready to dispense both discipline and a secret satisfaction disguised as holy duty.

Today was Agnes' day of service – a day some might call cruel, but which Agnes viewed as a sacred duty. Agnes squeezed her eyes shut, picturing young Sister Clara kneeling on the cold stone floor, her back bare and vulnerable. A flicker of something akin to pity sparked within Agnes, quickly extinguished by the righteous fire that always followed. Clara's disobedience, her innocent defiance, was a cancer that needed burning away.

"Pride," Agnes muttered, the word is a weapon against the guilt.

"Pride is the devil's snare," and Clara was teetering on the edge. This, this was an act of love, a harsh but necessary pruning to ensure her soul wouldn't be consumed by the flames of vanity. The justification, though practiced, felt hollow on her tongue.

Agnes yearned for the pure, selfless devotion she believed guided her actions. But beneath the surface, a different truth writhed. The rhythmic sting of the birch against flesh, the choked sobs of repentance – this was a perverse pleasure, a secret addiction Agnes desperately tried to cloak in piety. Taking a deep breath, Agnes rapped sharply on the door. The anticipation was almost unbearable, a sickening mix of guilt and the thrill that made her fingers itch for the cool touch of the polished wood.

"Sister Clara," she called out, her voice firm but laced with a tremor she couldn't quite control.

"Prepare yourself for the time for penance has arrived." Her gaze flicked to the worn crucifix hanging at her waist.

"Forgive me, Father," she mumbled, the words a desperate plea lost in the echo of the hallway. "Guide my hand, and let this pain cleanse her soul. May it be a crucible that forges her faith, a testament to your unwavering love."

Chapter 2
A Cold Whisper of Comfort

~*~

A tremor ran through the weathered oak door, followed by the sharp rap that sent a jolt through Sister Clara. Her heart hammered a frantic rhythm against her ribs, a caged bird desperate for escape. She squeezed her eyes shut, the familiar taste of fear flooding her mouth. Today was the day. The day Sister Agnes, with her starched smile and eyes that held a glint of something far from kindness, would visit her wrath upon Clara's perceived transgressions. The birch rod, a constant threat that hung heavy in the air, promised a searing pain Clara knew all too well. But amidst the terror, a different voice whispered within her, a voice both gentle and strangely comforting. It wasn't a voice Clara could identify, yet it felt oddly familiar, a forgotten melody from a childhood dream.

"The pain is real, little one," it soothed, "but it cannot be helped. This is a test; a crucible you must endure."

Clara flinched, a shiver racking her thin frame. Endure? It felt less like a test and more like a cruel and unjust punishment.

"There is solace, however," the voice continued, a soft warmth spreading through Clara despite the approaching ordeal. "Beyond this veil of pain lies an existence you cannot yet comprehend. A place where your body and mind will be healed, where the pain will stop, and the scars will vanish like smoke."

The image of a world free from pain, a world where cruelty holds no power, sparked a flicker of hope within Clara. Was this just wishful thinking, or a glimpse of a truth yet to be revealed?

The voice continued, its words weaving a tapestry of peace and a strange sense of anticipation. "This life is but a fleeting moment. The true journey awaits, a journey where the good you've nurtured will blossom, and the wrongs inflicted upon you will be balanced."

Clara took a shaky breath, a newfound resolve firming in her chest. Perhaps the pain was inevitable, but it wouldn't define her. There was something beyond, a promise of a world where the scales of justice would finally tip in her favour. Just then, another sharp rap echoed on the door, shattering the fragile bubble of hope.

Sister Agnes' voice, laced with a chilling piety, called out: "Sister Clara, prepare yourself for the time for penance has arrived."

Tears welled up in Clara's eyes, but they weren't just tears of fear. They were tears mingled with a flicker of defiance and a newfound hope for a brighter existence beyond the pain that awaited. The first blow landed with a sickening thud that stole the air from Clara's lungs. A white-hot starburst erupted across her back, a searing supernova of pain that sent her world reeling. This agony was a monstrous thing, a writhing serpent coiling around her spine, squeezing the breath from her and twisting her insides into knots. Old wounds, hidden beneath the scratchy wool, split open with a wet, tearing sensation that had her gagging. As Clara knelt on that hard stone floor, memories started flooding back, a tidal wave of terror and humiliation. The coppery tang that filled her mouth wasn't new. It was the echo of the last beating, the taste of her own blood that had mingled with the dust motes dancing in the weak light. The memory of that taste, a grotesque communion with her own suffering, intensified the present agony thousand fold. Tears, hot and stinging, welled in her eyes, blurring the world into a watercolour nightmare. Her body, a temple a moment ago, was now a ravaged landscape, each lash of the rod a fresh earthquake that sent tremors of agony rippling through her, triggering aftershocks of the past torment.

The voice, undeniably angelic, carried a power that defied explanation. As Agnes continued her brutal ministrations, the birch rod, a metronome keeping time with Clara's ragged breaths, the angelic voice whispered tales of unimaginable beauty. It spoke of rolling meadows painted with flowers the colour of twilight, and crystal-clear rivers flowing through landscapes sculpted from pure light. With each word, the physical agony receded, replaced by a breath-taking panorama unfolding within Clara's mind. The voice described a world where kindness bloomed like wildflowers, a world where every living thing hummed with an inner peace. It was a stark contrast to the cold, stone floor beneath Clara's knees and the sting of betrayal that burned hotter than the welts forming on her back.

As Clara stumbled in and out of consciousness, the sound of that angelic voice lulled Clara into a state of trance. It wasn't a blissful oblivion, but a focused awareness where the physical pain became a distant echo. It was as if the voice was weaving a cocoon of comfort around her, a temporary haven where Agnes' cruelty held no power. The rhythmic blows continued, a dull counterpoint to the symphony playing within Clara's head. But with each strike, the voice grew stronger, it's melody morphing into a hymn of resilience and hope. The words, though indistinct, carried a profound message: the pain was temporary, but the strength she found within would remain.

As the final blow landed, a heavy silence descended. Agnes, her face flushed with exertion, finally stepped back. Clara remained on her knees, eyes closed, a faint smile playing on her lips. The angelic voice lingered for a moment longer, a warm caress before fading into the air. When Clara finally opened her eyes, the world seemed to shimmer. The familiar confines of the room were tinged with an ethereal glow, a remnant of the celestial vision. She looked up at Agnes, no longer with fear, but with a newfound clarity. The pain throbbed in her back, a dull ache, but it was insignificant compared to the glimmer of hope that now flickered within her. The beating was over, but Clara knew this wasn't the end. Something fundamental had shifted within her. The angel's voice, a whisper of another reality, had shown her a glimpse of a world where the scales of justice would finally be balanced. And for the first time, Clara wasn't afraid of what awaited her beyond the veil of life.

Chapter 3
A Whisper of Rebellion

~*~

Clara pushed herself to her feet, a wave of dizziness washing over her. The world tilted slightly, but she clung to the edge of her bed, her gaze fixed on Sister Agnes. The older nun stood stiffly, the birch rod clutched possessively in her hand, blood covered the rod and her tunic, she wore a mask of righteous indignation on her face. Agnes had expected tears, and pleas for forgiveness, the familiar litany of apologies and self-abasement that followed her punishments. But what she saw instead was a sight that sent a tremor of unease through her – a flicker of defiance in Clara's eyes, a small, knowing smile playing on her lips.

"Thank you, Sister Agnes," Clara said, her voice surprisingly steady despite the tremor that ran through her body.

The words came out soft, almost gentle, but Agnes detected a subtle edge, a newfound strength that hadn't been there before.

Agnes blinked, momentarily thrown off balance.

"Thank you?" she echoed; her voice laced with suspicion.

"Yes, thank you," Clara repeated, taking a tentative step forward. "For reminding me of what truly matters – faith, not fear."

Agnes' hand tightened around the birch rod. The unexpected turn of events unsettled her. Clara had always been a pliable student, easily moulded by fear and piety. This newfound defiance was a challenge to her authority, a subtle rebellion that couldn't be ignored.

"What are you rambling about, child?" Agnes snapped, her voice regaining its usual sternness.

"About the truth, Sister Agnes," Clara continued, her voice gaining strength with each word. "The truth that hides behind your facade of piety. The truth about the suffering you inflict under the guise of penance."

Agnes' face flushed crimson. The accusation hung heavy in the air, a stark contrast to the whispered reassurances of the angelic voice that still echoed faintly within Clara's mind.

"Don't be blasphemous, child!" Agnes hissed, taking a threatening step forward. "You will confess your sins, and I will deliver the appropriate punishment!"

But Clara stood her ground, her gaze unwavering. The pain in her back throbbed with a dull ache, but it was overshadowed by a burning resolve.

"There's more to be punished than youthful disobedience, Sister Agnes," she said, her voice firm.

"And who are you to judge that?" Agnes shouted; her voice laced with a hint of desperation.

"I am a witness," Clara declared, her voice ringing with newfound authority. "A witness to the cruelty that festers within these very walls. A witness to the secrets you and the other elders have buried for far too long."

Agnes' face contorted in a mixture of anger and fear. The accusation was a dangerous one, a crack in the carefully constructed facade of the convent.

"Lies!" Agnes roared, lunging forward as if to silence Clara.

But Clara remained unfazed.

"Lies that need to be exposed," she countered, her voice a steady whisper. "I may have endured your punishment, Sister Agnes, but I will not be silenced. I will see Mother Superior. I will tell her everything."

The mention of Mother Superior gave Agnes pause. The elderly leader, though frail, was known for her unwavering sense of justice. The thought of her scrutinizing convent practices, of potentially uncovering the truth about Agnes and the other elders, sent a shiver down Agnes' spine.

Clara saw the flicker of fear in Agnes' eyes, and a surge of triumph coursed through her. The angelic voice may have offered comfort, but it was her own inner strength, awakened by the ordeal, that had given her this voice.

Agnes opened her mouth to protest, but Clara cut her off.

"Help me to Mother Superior, Sister Agnes," she said, her voice surprisingly firm. "It's time the truth came to light."

Silence hung heavy in the air. Agnes stared at Clara, her face a mask of conflicting emotions. The power dynamic had shifted in that small, confined space. Clara, the once-obedient novice, now stood before her as an accuser, her newfound courage a weapon more potent than any birch rod. Agnes knew she had a choice to make. Silence Clara and risk the truth being exposed or acquiesce and face the potential consequences of Mother Superior's investigation. A long moment stretched between them, the weight of the convent's secrets hanging heavy in the air.

Chapter 4
Echoes of Another World

~*~

The world shimmered around Clara. The familiar austerity of the convent cell blurred at the edges, replaced by fleeting glimpses of landscapes that defied earthly logic. Rolling hills carpeted with flowers in impossible shades bloomed before her, while crystal-clear rivers flowed through valleys sculpted from pure light. The air itself carried the faint melody the angelic voice had woven during her ordeal, a melody that now resonated within her very soul. It wasn't a complete vision, but rather a series of impressions, whispers of another reality that lingered on the periphery of her consciousness. The memory of the pain, a dull throb in her back, seemed insignificant compared to the breath-taking beauty she had glimpsed. Clara looked up at Sister Agnes, the anger and defiance momentarily forgotten.

"Did you see it too?" Clara rasped, her voice a threadbare whisper, barely audible over the pounding in her ears. It was a question loaded with a strange serenity, a stark contrast to the raw agony etched on her face. "Did you see the … the other world?"

Agnes, for the first time, faltered. The practiced mask of piety slipped a fraction, revealing a flicker of something akin to ... fear? Was it possible? Could this broken girl, kneeling in a pool of her own blood, have glimpsed what Agnes herself had spent years desperately trying to erase from her mind – the echo of an afterlife, a realm of celestial choirs and starlit whispers?

A part of Agnes scoffed. Perhaps it was the beating, the sheer intensity of the pain driving Clara to feverish delirium. It had to be. Yet, another, more insidious part of Agnes couldn't shake the memory of her own childhood visions – fleeting glimpses of a world bathed in celestial light, a world Agnes had been conditioned to believe was a childish fantasy, a mere trick of the mind.

The weight of years of suppressed longing slammed into Agnes with the force of a battering ram. Here, kneeling before her, was a young woman who, in the throes of unimaginable pain, had somehow accessed a reality Agnes had spent a lifetime denying. The injustice of it all, the bitter sting of envy, threatened to choke her. How dare this girl, this victim of Agnes' twisted devotion, see what Agnes herself could not?

Agnes forced a harsh laugh, a brittle sound that echoed hollowly in the cold stone room.

"See what, child? You've taken a hard blow to the head. Take it from me," assured Agnes, "there are no other worlds, only the one we suffer in."

But even as the words left her lips, Agnes couldn't erase the doubt that flickered in her eyes, a tiny spark of rebellion against the ironclad control she'd built around her own faith.

"Nonsense, child," she said, her voice clipped. "Rest will clear your delusions."

But Clara wasn't convinced. The memory of that voice, so vivid and powerful in her head, refused to fade. It was more than just a dream, an undeniable glimpse of something far greater. A world where the pain she endured held no power, a world where the scales of justice would finally tip in her favour. Suddenly, the urgency of her mission returned. This vision, this glimpse of the afterlife, wasn't just a source of comfort. It was a testament to a truth that needed to be brought to light. The truth about the hypocrisy that festered within the convent walls, the truth about the suffering inflicted in the name of faith. Clara straightened her back, ignoring the ache that pulsed with every movement.

"Whether you believe me or not, Sister Agnes," she said, her voice firm, "the truth will come out. I will see Mother Superior, and I will tell her everything."

The journey to Mother Superior's quarters felt like an eternity. Each step sent a fresh wave of agony radiating through Clara's back. The makeshift bandage fashioned from a torn scrap of her sleepwear did little to contain the crimson tide that seeped through her thin tunic, staining the worn fabric a gruesome red. With each laboured breath, that metallic taste filled her mouth. The dizziness that had threatened to consume her after the beating had receded, replaced by a dull ache that throbbed with a relentless rhythm. Gasping for air, Clara clung to the rough stone wall for support, her vision blurring at the edges. Every step taken, every whispered conversation that drifted through the halls, seemed amplified in her heightened state. The faces of other nuns passed before her eyes – some averted, some filled with a morbid curiosity, none reaching out to offer aid. Their silence, Clara realised with a bitter pang, was as deafening as Agnes' cruelty. Agnes remained silent, her gaze fixed on Clara with a mixture of fear and something that could almost be interpreted as ... respect? Perhaps the glimpse of defiance, the unexpected strength Clara had displayed, had shaken Agnes more than she cared to admit. The silence stretched for a moment, thick with unspoken tension.

Then, with a sigh that seemed to carry the weight of years of buried secrets, Agnes spoke, "Very well, child," she said, her voice resigned. "We shall see Mother Superior. But be warned, the path you walk may not be as easy as you think."

Clara met her gaze, a flicker of doubt momentarily crossing her eyes. The vision of the afterlife offered solace, a promise of a world beyond pain. However, the journey to reach that world, the secrets she was about to expose, still lay shrouded in uncertainty.

Chapter 5
A Price for Silence

~*~

Finally, she reached the heavy oak door that marked Mother Superior's quarters. Mustering the last vestiges of her strength, she raised a shaking hand and knocked. The sound echoed through the hallway, a frail plea for justice amidst the oppressive silence of the convent. A long moment dragged by before the door creaked open, revealing a figure cloaked in black. Mother Superior, a woman whose wrinkles seemed etched by the very weight of her responsibility, opened the very heavy oak door, and a figure stumbled into the room and into Mother Superior's arms. It took a moment for her aged eyes to adjust, but when they did, a gasp escaped her lips. Standing before her wasn't a nun, but a spectre. Sister Clara, her once pristine white habit now a canvas of crimson stains, swayed precariously. Her face, pale and drawn, bore the unmistakable marks of violence, a split lip, a raw welt forming above her eye and blood everywhere. Yet, it was the defiance in her bloodshot eyes that truly shocked Mother Superior. Clara hesitated for a moment, her gaze flitting across the bloodstains marring her tunic. The pain was a constant presence, a dull throb that radiated from every welt and bruise on her back. She knew the journey here had taken its toll, but she wouldn't back down now, determined to see her fight for justice through to the very end.

"Sister Clara," she rasped, her voice like dry leaves rustling in the wind.

The normally composed woman found herself struggling for words. The implications of Clara's state were horrifying. These weren't wounds from a tumble or a minor injury from a wayward tool, they looked like a deliberate act of violence, perpetrated on one of her sisters within the very walls of the monastery. "What brings you to my doorstep in such a state?" The question came out a whisper as she was unable to comprehend who would do such a thing.

The room spun, a sickening waltz with nausea as Clara pushed herself upright. Every muscle in her body screamed in protest, a chorus of agony conducted by the throbbing pain in her back. Yet, through the haze of suffering, a single, burning ember of defiance remained.

"Mother Superior," she rasped, the words scraping raw against her throat like sandpaper.

Tears welled in her eyes, blurring the already distorted image of the room. But they weren't tears of weakness, not anymore. They were a desperate wellspring of hope, a silent plea for the woman who held the power to end this nightmare.

"I stand before you, Mother," Clara continued, her voice gaining a threadbare strength with each ragged breath. Blood caked her lip, a crimson stain mirroring the inferno burning within her, her voice, barely a whisper above a sob, cracked with emotion. "We are your daughters, you vowed to protect us, yet we suffer every day, and you stood by and watched.

"You knew, Mother Superior," Clara said, her voice gaining strength despite the throbbing pain. "You and the elders, you all knew. Yet you chose to look away, to let Agnes become your … your instrument of discipline."

Clara swayed, the weight of her ordeal threatening to pull her under. But with a final surge of defiance, she locked eyes with the Mother Superior.

"I beg of you, Mother," she pleaded, the raw vulnerability in her voice a stark contrast to the steely glint in her eyes. "Hear my words. End this suffering. Let the light of truth banish the darkness that has taken root within this sacred place."

Mother Superior's heart hammered against her ribs. Clara's words, though barely audible, were a thunderclap in that quiet room. The stain on her habit wasn't just blood, it was a stain on the very foundation of the monastery, a chilling accusation against one of their own. This wasn't a simple accident or a misunderstanding. The sheer volume of blood spoke volumes – Clara had been beaten, and not for the first time. The realisation hit Mother Superior with the force of a battering ram. This wasn't some outsider, this was a wolf in sheep's clothing, a predator disguised as a shepherd. And the weight of that knowledge settled on her shoulders like a leaden cloak.

Clara took a deep breath, the pain a searing reminder of what she was about to reveal. She spoke of the beatings, of Agnes' twisted sense of piety, and the way she used religion as a weapon to inflict pain on young and innocent girls. She spoke of the other nuns, the ones who knew and chose not to act, the ones who, through their silence, became complicit in Agnes' cruelty. She spoke of the elders, the ones who not only turned a blind eye but who encouraged Agnes' twisted methods, believing the suffering inflicted was somehow strengthening these young souls. Mother Superior listened in stony silence, her face an unreadable mask. Each horrifying detail Clara uttered, seemed to etch a new line upon her weathered skin. When Clara finished, a suffocating silence descended upon the room.

"And you believe I did nothing?" Mother Superior finally spoke, her voice laced with a dangerous undercurrent. "That I, the leader of this convent, allowed such barbarity to flourish under my very nose?"

Clara flinched, torn between defiance and a creeping sense of dread. Mother Superior's calm facade seemed like a thin veil barely concealing a storm of emotions.

Clara hesitated for a moment, her gaze flitting across the bloodstains marring her tunic. The pain was a constant presence, a dull throb that radiated from every welt and bruise on her back. She knew the journey here had taken its toll, but she wouldn't back down now. Taking a shaky step forward, she crossed the threshold, determined to see her fight for justice through to the very end.

Chapter 6
The Price of Inaction

~*~

The heavy oak door swung shut with a finality that echoed through the dimly lit chamber. Clara, her vision swimming from the exertion and loss of blood, barely registered the movement. All her attention was focused on Mother Superior, a frail figure silhouetted against the single flickering candle on the desk. A tense silence stretched between them, broken only by Clara's ragged breaths. It wasn't the silence of contemplation, but the heavy silence of a storm brewing just beneath the surface. Finally, Mother Superior spoke, her voice laced with a weariness that belied the steely glint in her eyes.

"Child," she rasped, "you understand the consequences of your accusations, don't you? The scandal it would bring upon the convent, the whispers that would stain our reputation."

Clara met her gaze, a newfound strength flickering in her own eyes.

"Justice has no price tag, Mother Superior," she countered, her voice surprisingly steady despite the pulsing pain in her back. "And the truth, however ugly, will eventually come to light."

"Justice?" Mother Superior scoffed, the sound brittle and humourless. "There is no justice in earthly matters, child. Only chaos and disorder."

"There may be no justice here," Clara agreed, her voice gaining conviction. "But there's a reckoning to come. A place where deeds, both good and evil, find their true weight."

A flicker of unease crossed Mother Superior's face. Then, with a sharp rap on the heavy oak desk, she summoned the elders. The door creaked open once again, allowing a group of weathered figures, their faces etched with a lifetime of pious pronouncements and buried secrets, to file into the room. Their gaze fell upon Clara, a mixture of curiosity and unease clouding their features. Clara, fuelled by a sudden surge of adrenaline, met their stares head-on. She recounted the details of her ordeal, the methodical brutality of the beatings, and the sickening hypocrisy that cloaked Agnes' actions. She spoke of their silence, their complicity, their belief that Agnes' cruelty somehow served a higher purpose. As the elders listened, their faces seemed to drain of colour. The weight of their inaction, the consequences of their misguided faith in Agnes' twisted methods, seemed to settle upon them like a shroud. They exchanged nervous glances, their once-assured posture crumbling under the weight of Clara's accusations.

"You knew," Clara pressed, her voice a ragged whisper. "You all knew and did nothing. Now, you will have to stand before your maker and explain."

A tremor of fear passed through the group. The afterlife, a realm they had spent their lives preparing their charges for, was suddenly a looming reality with terrifying implications.

But before any of them could voice their anxieties, Clara continued, her words tinged with a strange sense of serenity.

"But know this," she said, her voice gaining strength. "Death is not the end. It is merely a passage to another dimension, a world where the scales of justice finally tip in favour of the wronged."

Clara described the vision, the glimpses of an afterlife she had experienced during the beating – the rolling meadows painted with impossible flowers, the rivers of pure light. It wasn't a place of punishment, but a world of unimaginable beauty, where her suffering would find solace and where Agnes would face the true consequences of her actions. The elders listened in stunned silence, their rigid belief in a more traditional and harsher afterlife challenged by Clara's vivid description. A flicker of hope, a desperate yearning for this promised beauty, flickered in their eyes. Mother Superior, her face an unreadable mask, studied Clara intently. Could this young novice, bloodied and battered yet radiating a strange aura of peace, be right? Was there truly more to existence than the rigid doctrines they had spent their lives upholding?

Clara's voice, weakened but resolute, echoed in the dimly lit chamber: "This is not the end," she declared, her words holding a weight that transcended her physical pain. "It is a new beginning."

Clara's vision of the afterlife has shaken the very foundation of the elders' beliefs. While the immediate consequences of her actions remain uncertain, a seed of doubt has been planted, hinting at a reality beyond earthly justice and a more hopeful fate awaiting them all.

Chapter 7
Beyond the Veil

~*~

The acrid tang of blood-filled Clara's mouth, a metallic counterpoint to the symphony of pain that had become her existence. Through half-lidded eyes, she saw the perpetrators of her torture slink back into the shadows, their faces obscured but their cruelty etched into her memory.

"This world may be yours now," she rasped, her voice a bloody whisper, "but there is another to come. A divine reckoning where the Almighty will weigh our souls, and your wickedness will be laid bare."

Her voice, though weak, held a sliver of steel.

"The kindness I offered you, the mercy you cast aside, it will all be counted. And I, Clara, will be there to witness your descent into damnation."

A guttural scoff echoed from the darkness.

"There is no afterlife, only oblivion. Your pathetic god is a fairy-tale for the weak."

Clara coughed, a spray of crimson painting the dust at her feet. A wan smile tugged at the corner of her lips.

"Even if oblivion awaits, fear it, for it will be a paradise compared to the eternity of suffering reserved for those who revel in inflicting pain."

Her vision swam, the edges of reality blurring. Yet, through the haze, a strange clarity bloomed within her. This wasn't the end. It was merely a transition. With a final, rattling breath, Clara whispered a vow, not a plea, but a promise that chilled the unseen figures watching.

"I'll see you all there."

The world dissolved into a swirling vortex of light and shadow. Clara surrendered to the oblivion, a strange sense of peace washing over her. But then, just as the darkness threatened to consume her utterly, a flicker of warmth ignited within. A single ember, faint but persistent, refusing to be extinguished. Clara gasped, her eyes snapping open. But this wasn't the cold, damp earth she expected. Instead, she found herself suspended in an ethereal space, a breath-taking panorama of swirling constellations and stardust stretching out before her.

A voice, ancient and profound, resonated through the void, "Welcome, Clara, to the in-between."

Chapter 8
The Price of Conviction

~*~

The silence after Clara's final rasp was as heavy as the stones beneath their feet. The Elders and the Mother Superior shifted uncomfortably; the desert heat suddenly oppressive. The cruelty that had hardened their features moments ago had curdled into a sour unease. Elder Mathus, the oldest and most rigid, cleared his throat, the sound grating in the stillness.

"Her ... blasphemy ..." he began, his voice tight.

But even his usual conviction wavered.

Elder Amara, known for her pragmatism, scoffed. "She was a raving madwoman at the end. Ignore her ramblings."

Yet, her eyes darted nervously towards the horizon, as if searching for a sign, a rebuttal to Clara's chilling words.

The Mother Superior, usually meticulous with her notes, stared blankly at the empty parchment in her hand. Clara's words about an 'endless journey' and a 'next part of the story' echoed in her mind, a stark contrast to the carefully scripted history she'd been taught.

"But what if ..." Elder Elara, the youngest and most empathetic, dared to speak, her voice barely a whisper. "What if there is more? What if the stories we tell ourselves ..."

She didn't finish the sentence, the fear of heresy palpable. The others wouldn't dare voice it, but the seed of doubt had been planted. A lifetime of indoctrination was starting to crumble under the weight of a dying woman's conviction.

Mathus pounded his staff on the ground, a desperate attempt to regain control.

"We uphold the teachings! The Almighty will guide us!" But even his booming voice lacked its usual fervour.

Amara pursed her lips, her gaze hardening.

"Perhaps … a more … thorough interrogation was in order. How did she come to these … delusions?"

The question hung heavy in the air.

Had they, in their zeal to enforce their version of order, unwittingly created a heretic? Or had Clara, in her final moments, exposed a truth they'd conveniently ignored for generations? A single crow circled overhead, its harsh caw echoing in the vast emptiness. It seemed to mock their newfound uncertainty. As the sun dipped below the horizon, casting long, skeletal shadows across the wasteland, the Elders and the Mother Superior knew their world had shifted. Clara's death had left a void, not just in their ranks, but in the very foundation of their beliefs. The night stretched before them, vast and unknown, much like the fate that awaited them, a fate, Clara had promised, they would all face, together.

Chapter 9
Supper of Shadows

~*~

The days that followed Clara's death were a macabre dance of normalcy. Sister Agnes, pale and drawn, moved through the routines with a robotic efficiency. The Elders, once pillars of unwavering certainty, became shadows of their former selves. Gone was the booming authority in their voices, replaced by a hesitancy that bordered on fear. Elder Mathus, ever the disciplinarian, found himself flinching at raised voices, his punishments half-heartedly delivered. Elder Amara, the pragmatist, spent hours hunched over ancient texts, searching for answers that seemed to elude her. Even Elder Elara, the voice of reason, walked with a haunted look in her eyes. The seed of doubt Clara had sown had taken root, blossoming into a poisonous flower of disbelief. Sister Agnes, shrouded in her own guilt, observed this unravelling with a detached coldness. The woman she'd once blindly followed was gone, replaced by a bitter resentment. Perhaps, she thought, if the Elders had shown even a sliver of the compassion Clara preached, things wouldn't have come to this.

One evening, under the guise of a celebratory meal for 'restoring order', Agnes prepared a simple stew. It looked innocent enough, a familiar comfort food in the harsh desert life. But beneath the surface lurked a deadly secret. A poison, carefully procured, waited to claim its victims. As they sat around the rough-hewn table, the Elders, for the first time, seemed to truly see Agnes. Not the meek follower, but a woman honed by hardship, her eyes burning with a quiet fury. A tremor of unease ran through them, a premonition of something amiss.

"To a new beginning," Agnes raised her cup, her voice devoid of emotion.

The Elders echoed the toast, a hollow murmur escaping their lips.

They took a sip, the familiar warmth of the stew spreading through them. But soon, a subtle change. A tightness in the chest, a cold sweat breaking out on their foreheads. Panic flickered in their eyes, a stark contrast to the unwavering faith they once held. Agnes watched, a chilling smile playing on her lips.

"Perhaps, love isn't the only weapon," she whispered, her voice barely audible. "Sometimes, faith needs a little … persuasion."

One by one, the Elders crumpled to the floor, their faces contorted in a silent scream. The once revered leaders of the order, lay lifeless, their demise as swift as it was unexpected. Agnes rose, her eyes devoid of tears, and walked out into the night. The desert wind howled, carrying with it the chilling echo of a promise fulfilled – a twisted act of vengeance veiled as a poisoned supper.

Chapter 10
Desolation's Embrace

~*~

The relentless sun beat down on Agnes, turning the desert sand into a shimmering furnace. Every breath felt like a shard of glass in her raw throat. The Elders were gone, their faces a fading memory in the haze of her feverish mind. She had walked for days, the meagre supplies she grabbed a mockery of survival. Her once pristine robes hung in tatters, offering no protection from the scorching heat. Regret, a bitter bile, rose in her throat. The image of Clara, defiant even in death, haunted her. The love and compassion the woman preached seemed a cruel joke in this unforgiving landscape. Agnes stumbled, her legs weak and shaking. The once vibrant world had shrunk to a blur of shimmering mirages and the relentless, mocking sun. She had sought solace in the desert, a fitting punishment for her sins. Yet, even death seemed to elude her. The vultures, ever watchful, circled overhead, their guttural cries a constant reminder of the inevitable.

As the days bled into one another, Agnes' once-sharp mind dulled. The harsh beauty of the desert, once alien, now held a strange, macabre allure. Perhaps, it was a reflection of the desolation that had taken root within her. One evening, as the sun dipped below the horizon, painting the sky in fiery hues, Agnes finally collapsed. She felt a strange sense of peace, a surrender to the inevitable. The vultures, sensing their moment, swooped down, their dark forms blotting out the last slivers of light. There was no scream, no struggle. The desert claimed her, another nameless victim in its timeless embrace. In the silence that followed, only the wind whispered a mournful song, a lament for a soul consumed by vengeance and ultimately, consumed by the very world she sought to punish.

Agnes stumbled through the shimmering desert heat, her vision blurring with exhaustion. The vultures, ever-present harbingers of doom, circled lazily overhead. With a final, ragged breath, she crumpled onto the scorching sand, welcoming the oblivion she craved. But instead of darkness, a soft, cool breeze washed over her. As her eyes fluttered open, she found herself standing on a vast expanse of greyish-white sand. The air shimmered, obscuring everything beyond a few feet. Fear, cold and primal, coiled in her stomach. A faint rustling sound drew her attention. Three figures materialised from the swirling mist; their forms cloaked in a soft, unearthly light. As they approached, Agnes recognised them with a jolt. The Elders – their faces etched with neither anger nor malice, but a curious emptiness.

"Agnes," Elder Mathus spoke, his voice devoid of the booming authority she remembered. "We have been waiting."

Agnes wanted to scream, to lash out at them for their cruelty, for their hypocrisy. But the words died in her throat, choked by a strange sense of powerlessness. Here, in this desolate purgatory, the past held no sway.

Chapter 11
A Song of Redemption

~*~

Just then, a small figure emerged from the mist. A boy, no older than ten, with eyes that held an ageless wisdom. He was dressed in a simple white tunic, his bare feet leaving no imprint on the sand.

"Come," he said, his voice a gentle chime. "It is time to follow the path."

Without a word, the Elders followed the boy, their forms trailing behind him like wisps of smoke. Agnes hesitated, her heart pounding against her ribs. Was this another trick, another torment?

"Do not be afraid," the boy said, turning back as if sensing her trepidation. "There is no judgment here, only ... waiting."

With a deep breath, Agnes stepped forward, the sand cool and surprisingly soft beneath her bare feet. The boy led them deeper into the swirling mist, the path ahead uncertain. As they walked, the greyish landscape slowly transformed. The air shimmered, revealing patches of vibrant colour – verdant fields, crystalline waterfalls, and towering trees laden with exotic fruits. The oppressive silence gave way to a symphony of birdsong and the gentle murmur of a nearby stream. Agnes gasped. It was a paradise beyond anything she could have imagined. Lush meadows stretched as far as the eye could see, bathed in a golden light that seemed to emanate from everywhere and nowhere at once.

"Where ... where are we?" Agnes stammered; her voice rough with disuse.

The boy smiled, a hint of sadness in his eyes.

"This is just the beginning," he said. "A taste of what awaits those who have lived a life of ... potential."

His words hung heavy in the air. Agnes stared at the idyllic landscape, her mind reeling. This wasn't the hellfire she'd envisioned, nor the pearly gates of heaven. It was ... something else entirely. A place of waiting, a space for reflection before the next destination.

The boy turned and continued walking, the Elders trailing silently behind him. Agnes followed; her heart heavy with a newfound sense of uncertainty. The scorching desert and the vultures were gone, replaced by a beauty that left her breathless. Yet, a nagging question echoed in the vastness: Was this paradise? A reward? Or merely a waiting room for something far greater, or far worse? The journey had just begun, and Agnes, for the first time in a long time, was truly afraid of what awaited her at the end of this path.

Days, perhaps weeks, blurred into one another as they followed the young man, now appearing a youthful twenty years old. The greyish purgatory had fully dissolved, replaced by a breath-taking paradise. Sunlight, soft and warm, bathed the landscape, casting vibrant hues on meadows bursting with wildflowers. Crystal-clear streams gurgled merrily, punctuated by the joyous chirping of unseen birds. Agnes, the Elders silent at her side, couldn't shake off the strangeness of it all. The beauty was undeniable, yet it felt … incomplete. Like a perfectly painted stage waiting for the actors to arrive.

Chapter 12
Whispers on the Wind

~*~

One idyllic afternoon, as butterflies danced in the gentle breeze and animals frolicked in the meadows, a sound drifted through the air. A voice, faint at first, a mere whisper on the wind. They all stopped, straining to hear. It was a voice both familiar and strangely distant, tugging at Agnes's memory. The young man, ever silent until now, turned with a knowing smile.

"It is time," he said, his voice like the tinkling of a crystal stream.

He began to walk purposefully towards the source of the voice, his pace quickening. Agnes, her heart pounding with a mixture of dread and anticipation, followed closely. The Elders, their faces devoid of emotion but their eyes gleaming with a spark of curiosity, trailed behind. As they walked, the voice grew clearer. It was a woman's voice, melodic and warm, yet with a hint of underlying strength. A voice that sent a jolt through Agnes.

"Sister Clara?" she breathed, the name tumbling out on a wave of disbelief.

The vibrant landscape seemed to shimmer in acknowledgment. They crested a small hill, and there, bathed in the golden light, stood a figure. A woman turned to face them; her silhouette outlined against the sun-dappled meadows. Agnes's breath hitched. The woman's long, dark hair was unmistakable, as was the unwavering resolve in her stance. It was Clara, no doubt about it. Clara, alive and well. But something was different. Her robes, once simple and worn, now shimmered with an otherworldly light. Her eyes, once filled with quiet defiance, now held a wisdom that transcended the mortal realm.

Clara smiled, a radiant beam that chased away the shadows lingering in Agnes' heart.

"I have been waiting for you," she said, her voice filling the air like a comforting melody.

Agnes, overwhelmed with a torrent of emotions – relief, guilt, a desperate yearning for forgiveness – stumbled forward. The Elders, too, quickened their pace, their earlier stoicism replaced by a cautious curiosity. But before anyone could take another step, the young man, his smile fading into a serious expression, raised a hand.

"Not yet," he said, his voice echoing with gentle authority. "There is much to be done before you stand before the Maker."

Clara tilted her head, her gaze sweeping over each of them.

"Indeed," she agreed. "There are lessons learned, and perhaps, amends to be made."

A shiver ran down Agnes' spine. Lessons? Amends? The idyllic paradise now felt heavy with unspoken expectations. What awaited them here, in this beautiful yet unsettling purgatory? As the sun began its descent, casting long shadows across the meadows, Clara gestured towards a grove of trees laden with luminous fruits.

"Come," she said, her voice soft yet firm. "We have much to discuss."

Agnes followed; drawn by a force she couldn't explain. Perhaps this wasn't the final judgment she'd envisioned, but something far more complex. Here, in the presence of the woman she'd wronged, Agnes knew her journey towards redemption had truly begun.

Chapter 13
Unveiling the Maker

~*~

The colossal golden doors of the cathedral creaked open, revealing a vista that took Agnes's breath away. Sunlight streamed through stained-glass windows, casting rainbows across a vast, cavernous space. Rows upon rows of intricately carved pews stretched towards a central dais, where a single, massive throne of burnished gold awaited. Was this it? Heaven? Agnes, a knot of apprehension tightening in her stomach, couldn't shake the feeling that something was amiss.

They followed the young angel, who had guided them through the paradise-like purgatory, down the seemingly endless aisle. The silence in the cathedral was profound, broken only by the soft click of their footsteps on the polished marble floor.

As they finally reached the dais, Agnes felt an overwhelming sense of insignificance before the towering throne. The gold seemed to radiate an oppressive heat, almost mocking.

"Wait here," the angel said, her voice barely a whisper before dissolving into a shimmering light.

They stood awkwardly, the Elders shifting their weight from one foot to the other. Agnes, her mind racing, couldn't help but vocalise the question that hung heavy in the air.

"Where ... where is the Maker?"

A deep, resonant voice boomed from somewhere within the cathedral, seemingly emanating from everywhere at once.

"Patience, my children. The wait is almost over."

The floor trembled subtly, and the air shimmered.

A blinding light erupted from behind the golden throne, forcing them to shield their eyes. When the light subsided, Agnes gasped.

Gone was the opulent chair. In its place stood a figure cloaked in pure white light. The radiance was so intense, they could only make out the silhouette – a woman with a gentle, familiar posture. Clara.

The air crackled with a strange energy as Clara, or whoever this luminous being was, spoke, "Welcome, children." Her voice echoed, still powerful yet infused with an otherworldly kindness.

Agnes stumbled back; disbelief etched on her face.

"Clara? But ... but that's impossible!"

Clara, the radiant figure, smiled. A smile that somehow managed to radiate warmth and understanding through the blinding light.

"There are many names I have worn throughout the ages," she said, her voice a soothing melody. "But my purpose has always remained the same – to guide you towards love, compassion, and forgiveness."

"You ..." Agnes stammered, the truth dawning on her with agonising slowness. "You are ... the Maker?"

Clara stepped down from the dais, the light dimming slightly, allowing them to see her form more clearly. Yes, it was the same woman, her features softened by the ethereal glow – a face etched in Agnes's memory by both fear and a flicker of something she couldn't quite place, a flicker of something … divine.

"Every action has a reaction," Clara continued, her voice filled with a quiet sorrow. "And in your zeal, you lost sight of the very foundation of my teachings. You inflicted suffering in my name, causing pain to the very souls I seek to embrace."

The Elders, their faces ashen, looked ready to crumble. Agnes, tears welling in her eyes, sank to her knees. The enormity of her actions, the cruelty she'd justified in the name of a twisted faith, washed over her like a tidal wave.

"But," Clara continued, her voice softening, "there is always a chance for redemption. You have faced your mistakes. You have felt the consequences of your choices."

She looked at each of them in turn, her gaze lingering on Agnes a moment longer.

"Now, the true test begins. Here, in this place between worlds, you have a chance to show if you have truly learned the meaning of love."

The revelation, the sheer audacity of it, left Agnes speechless. The Maker, the all-powerful being she'd worshipped, wasn't a wrathful judge but a figure of compassion, a being who walked among them, disguised as the very person they'd condemned. Clara, or the Maker, or whoever this luminous being truly was, had shown them a glimpse of paradise, a taste of what could have been. Now, it was up to them to prove they were worthy – not of some opulent heaven, but of something far more profound: the ability to spread love and understanding in the world they were about to return to. The vast cathedral, once a symbol of power and authority, now felt strangely intimate. The weight of judgment had shifted, replaced by the daunting prospect of a new beginning. Agnes knew, with a heavy heart, that the true test wasn't here, bathed in the light of their Maker. It was waiting for them back on Earth, amidst the chaos and conflict of the mortal world.

Chapter 14
Whispers of the Soul

~*~

The cathedral, once a monument to earthly grandeur, now stood bathed in a soft, ethereal light. Gone were the golden opulence and the oppressive weight of expectation. In their place, a single flickering candle cast dancing shadows on the stark white walls. Before them stood Clara, or perhaps something more, an embodiment of the divine cloaked in a shimmering white radiance. Her voice, when she spoke, echoed with the gentle cadence of wind chimes, carrying a profound truth.

"You stand at the crossroads of your journey," she began, her gaze sweeping over Agnes and the Elders. "A lifetime of actions, both grand and seemingly trivial, have led you here. Here, where the veil between worlds is thin, you are offered a glimpse into the true nature of existence."

As she spoke, the room seemed to shift, the floor transforming into a vast, star-strewn expanse. A million points of light twinkled above, each representing a soul, each one a reflection of choices made, and paths taken.

"Every decision, every act of cruelty or kindness," Clara continued, "leaves an indelible mark on your soul. It is the very essence of who you are, the fuel that feeds your spirit."

Agnes, her eyes wide with understanding, thought back to her life in the monastery. The harsh punishments, the unwavering belief in the righteousness of their actions. It felt like a lifetime ago, yet the memory resonated with a chilling clarity.

"We were only following orders," Elder Mathus croaked, his voice hollow. "We were upholding the teachings."

A flicker of sadness crossed Clara's luminous features.

"Free will," she said, the words echoing through the vastness, "is the greatest gift bestowed upon you. It is the power to choose love over hate, compassion over cruelty."

With a wave of her hand, a scene unfolded before them. A bustling marketplace, filled with the cacophony of everyday life. A young boy, his face etched with hunger, reached out to a well-dressed merchant, begging for a scrap of food. The merchant, his face twisted in disgust, shooed the boy away with a callous remark. Agnes watched, the memory of Sister Clara's pleas for kindness burning in her mind. Shame clawed at her as she realised how often they had turned a blind eye to suffering, justifying their actions with the cold comfort of obedience. The scene shifted. Now, a lone figure walked through a war-torn landscape, offering solace to the wounded and tending to the dying. The figure, bathed in a gentle light, resembled Clara, yet also held a timeless quality.

"This is the path of love," Clara's voice whispered. "The path that nourishes the soul and brings light to those around you."

Another scene played out – a brutal execution, screams echoing through the night. Agnes flinched, recognising the twisted faces of herself and the Elders. The memory hung heavy, a stark reminder of the darkness they had sown.

"This is the path of hate," Clara said, her voice filled with sorrow. "A path that weighs heavy upon the soul, draining it of its essence."

The candle flickered, the flame responding to the weight of their choices. As images of cruelty and compassion danced before them, the light grew dimmer, the shadows lengthening.

"Each choice you make," Clara continued, "adds a feather to your wings. Feathers of love lift you towards the light, while those of cruelty bind you to the earth. When the flame of your life finally flickers, it will be the weight of these feathers that determines your fate."

Chapter 15
A Newfound Vulnerability

~*~

The air crackled with unspoken truths. The punishment wasn't a fiery hell or heavenly bliss, but the burden they carried within. The pain they inflicted would become a weight, dragging them down, while acts of compassion would provide the lift to rise above. Agnes, tears streaming down her face, looked at the flickering candle. The choice, she understood with a heart-wrenching clarity, wasn't about a final judgment. It was about the journey itself, a constant struggle between darkness and light, a decision made with every breath. And as they stood there, bathed in the fading light, the truth resonated: true redemption wasn't a destination, but a lifelong pursuit, a path paved with love, compassion, and the conscious choice to rise above the darkness that threatened to consume them.

As the sun dipped below the horizon, painting the sky in breath-taking hues of orange and pink, Agnes knew, with a certainty that warmed her soul, that even the smallest act of compassion could light the way, not just for others, but for oneself as well. It was a journey of constant learning, of stumbles and triumphs, a journey filled with tears, both of pain and of a love so profound it brought a grown man to his knees. It was a journey worth taking, a journey she would continue, feather by feather, until her very last breath. And in the quiet moments, when the weight of her past threatened to overwhelm, Agnes would close her eyes and see him again. The man on the cross, his body broken, hands and feet tethered, a spear wound marring his flesh.

Yet, from his lips came a whisper, a plea for forgiveness – "For they do not know what they do."

In those words, Agnes found not just a call for compassion, but a profound truth. Forgiveness wasn't a gift for the wicked, but a path for the lost, a way to lighten the burden they carried. And perhaps, just perhaps, the greatest act of love wasn't just showing kindness to others, but finding the strength to forgive oneself, feather by feather, until the burden of the past finally lifted, allowing the soul to truly fly. The blinding light receded, replaced by the familiar roughness of the wooden pews. Agnes blinked, adjusting to the dimness of the old monastery chapel. It wasn't paradise, nor was it fire and brimstone. It was simply … their world. Reality felt raw, the weight of their choices pressing down on them. The Elders, their faces etched with a newfound vulnerability, shuffled out of the chapel. Agnes lingered; her eyes drawn to the flickering candle on the altar. It burned low, a reminder of the delicate balance they now carried within. A sudden commotion from the courtyard pierced the quiet. Laughter, loud and unruly, shattered the peace. Agnes sighed, the memories of the classroom flooding back. This wasn't paradise, but it was her new battleground.

She stepped outside, the boisterous energy of the children hitting her like a wave. They were a motley crew, some with mischievous smiles, others with eyes clouded by anger and neglect. A younger version of herself, perhaps. Agnes felt a familiar pang of frustration. This wasn't the grand redemption she'd envisioned. No choirs of angels, no streets paved with gold. Just a chaotic classroom, filled with the noise of childhood. But then, as she looked closer, a flicker of something else caught her eye. A small girl, huddled in a corner, ostracised by the others. A tear traced a glistening path down her cheek.

In that moment, a vision flooded Agnes's mind. A vision from the vast, star-strewn expanse – the weightless joy of lifting another soul with an act of kindness. The agonising burden of choosing hate. A wave of emotion washed over her – regret, shame, and a newfound resolve. This wasn't a punishment; it was an opportunity. An opportunity to choose a different path, feather by feather. With a deep breath, Agnes walked towards the girl. The classroom may not have been paradise, but it was her new world, and she, it's unlikely guardian angel.

~*~

Years later, Agnes stood by the window, watching the sun set over the familiar landscape of the monastery. Her classroom was no longer a battleground, but a haven. The children, once unruly, were now filled with a curiosity for the world. A young man, his eyes filled with a newfound kindness, approached her. He was once the defiant boy who had led the rebellion in her class. Now, he held a book in his hand, a book on philosophy.

"Thank you," he said, his voice thick with emotion. "Thank you for showing me there's another way."

A single tear rolled down Agnes' cheek, a tear that wasn't of sadness, but of profound understanding and pure joy, seeing how this once rebellious young lad had turned into a completely different person. The journey was long, the weight of the past a constant companion. But the warmth in the young man's eyes, the echo of kindness in his voice – that was the reward. That was the proof that, love, however hard-fought, always finds a way to bloom, even in the most unlikely of places.

As the sun dipped below the horizon, painting the sky in breath-taking hues of orange and pink, Agnes knew, with a certainty that warmed her soul, that even the smallest act of compassion could light the way, not just for others, but for oneself as well. It was a journey of constant learning, of stumbles and triumphs, a journey filled with tears, both of pain and of a love so profound it brought a grown man to his knees. It was a journey worth taking, a journey she would continue, feather by feather, until her very last breath. And in the quiet moments, when the weight of her past threatened to overwhelm, Agnes would close her eyes and see him again. The man on the cross, his body broken, hands and feet tethered, a spear wound marring his flesh. A tremor ran through Agnes, a ripple of understanding that echoed through the deepest chambers of her soul.

It wasn't just the raw emotion in the whispered plea, "For they do not know what they do," that struck her. It was a revelation, a divine spark igniting in the darkness she'd built within herself.

Forgiveness. It wasn't a weapon of the righteous, a tool to punish or belittle the wicked. It was a lifeline thrown to the lost, a shimmering bridge across the chasm of sin and regret. Each act of forgiveness, she realised with a gasp, wasn't just a gift for the transgressor, but a release for the one offering it. It was the loosening of a heavy chain, a feather gently unburdened from the weight of the past. Tears welled in Agnes' eyes, blurring the edges of the world. The weight of her own darkness, the burden of past actions, pressed down on her, threatening to crush her. Yet, within the despair, a flicker of hope ignited. Forgiveness, she now understood with a heart overflowing with a strange mix of sorrow and relief, wasn't just about extending compassion to others. It was the ultimate act of self-love – a feather-by-feather dismantling of the prison she'd built around her own soul.

This wasn't just about earthly redemption, but a celestial dance of liberation. With each act of forgiveness, a piece of the darkness would loosen its grip, allowing a sliver of light to pierce through. Perhaps, just perhaps, with enough forgiveness, enough feathers gently cast aside, her soul could finally take flight, soaring towards a future bathed in the celestial light of acceptance and grace.